SAFE IN THE ARK

AND OTHER BIBLE STORIES

Also available

Walking on Water and Other Bible Stories

SAFE IN THE ARK

AND OTHER BIBLE STORIES

ANNE ADENEY

ILLUSTRATED BY RUTH RIVERS

Orion
Children's Books

This edition first published in Great Britain in 2007
by Orion Children's Books
a division of the Orion Publishing Group Ltd
Orion House
5 Upper St Martin's Lane
London WC2H 9EA
An Hachette Livre UK Company

1 3 5 7 9 10 8 6 4 2

The stories in this volume were originally published as part of
The Biggest Bible Storybook, first published by Orion Children's Books in 2003

Text copyright © Anne Adeney 2003
Illustrations copyright © Ruth Rivers 2003

The rights of Anne Adeney and Ruth Rivers to be identified
as the author and illustrator of this work respectively have been asserted.

Designed by Louise Millar

A catalogue record for this book is available
from the British Library.

Printed by Printer Trento, Italy

ISBN 9 78 184255 601 6

www.orionbooks.co.uk

Contents

Introduction

I love to hear stories and to tell them too. The Bible is the biggest storybook in the whole world! It is really sixty-six different books all inside one cover, with thousands of stories, but I've picked out fifty of the very best from the Old Testament for you.

I'm sure you like to hear stories too. Children have listened to stories since time began and then told them to someone else; maybe their friends, or their brothers and sisters. Then when they grow up, they tell the stories to their own children. This book is full of children telling the stories they have heard or even telling about things they have seen with their own eyes.

The storytellers are all children from long ago, so their way of life was very different from ours. There were no cars in Bible times, or TVs or books like this to read. Children your age even had jobs. They helped look after the animals, usually sheep, goats and donkeys. They helped their parents in their work as fishermen, carpenters, weavers or brickmakers. But even though their way of life was different, they were still children, just like you. They liked to hear stories and to tell them, to laugh, joke, and play.

The stories were told over and over again and have been passed down through the ages. Maybe when you've heard one, you could tell it to someone else, to keep the stories moving through time. The children in this book loved hearing and telling these stories. I hope you do too.

Anne Adeney
Plymouth

EVA'S STORY

My name is Eva and I'm the grand-daughter of a goatherd. I live in the hills of Judah with my family.

'I wish I'd been there when the world was created!' I said. 'I wish I could have seen God make everything.'

'You're always wishing for something you can't have, Eva,' said my grand-mother, laughing. 'Why not just wish for a fig, like your brother? Anyway, there were no little girls around when God made the world. No grown-ups either, not even Adam and Eve.'

'Tell the story again, Grandmother!' I asked.

'I've no time for stories now, Eva!' said Grandmother, as she took up her strong stick. 'I must go and milk the goats and you must look after your little brother. You've heard the story often enough, why don't you be the storyteller and tell him?'

My brother was sitting outside our tent, eating the fig Grandmother had given him. I still remember that day when we sat together and I told Mo all the stories I knew about God creating the world. I told him a story for every year of my life. The first one was about the coming of light.

1
Creation of Light

Long, long ago, before the beginning of time, there was nothing except God. Then God made the heaven and the earth. He made heaven a bright, beautiful place. But the earth was dark and cold and empty. It didn't even have a shape.

So God decided that he wanted the earth to be a beautiful place as well. God can do *anything* at all, so he could create the world just as he wanted it. But the earth was as dark as could be, so on the very first day God said, 'Let there be light.'

Immediately light shone in the sky and some of the darkness went. But God is very wise. He knew that it would be just as bad to have all light as all darkness. So he kept some of the darkness. God said, 'I'll call the light *day* and the darkness *night*.' So that's how we got morning and evening. God looked at the day and the night that he had created and said, 'That is *good*!'

EVA'S STORY

'What happened next, Eva?' asked Mo.

'It's the story of what happened on the second day,' I said, 'when God made the sky. This is how he did it.'

2
Creation of the Sky

On the second day God looked at the earth. He could see it well now, because he'd created light. But all he could see was water. There was water everywhere. It covered the whole earth. So God said, 'There's too much water here, I need to separate it.'

Then God spoke and a huge blue space appeared above the waters covering the earth. 'I'll call this space *sky*,' said God.

There was still water above the earth, but God made big fluffy clouds to hold the water in the sky.

God looked at the sky and the clouds that he had created and said, 'That is *good*!'

EVA'S STORY

'What did God make next, Eva?' asked Mo.

'Well, it was the third day by then,' I said. 'There was day and night and sky and clouds, but there was no land for things to grow on. So next he had to create the land and the sea.'

3
Creation of the Land and Sea

God looked around the earth and he said, 'There's still too much water here. We need something different. I'm going to create some dry ground.'

So God spoke. That's all he had to do to make something happen. He just said, 'Let all the waters on the earth be gathered together,' and they were.

God looked at the waters and said, 'I'll call them *seas*.'

Then he could see all the dry ground sticking out between the seas. 'I'll call this dry ground *land*,' he said. God looked at the land and the seas and he was very pleased with what he had made.

God wanted plants to grow so he made soil to go on top of the land. He made rich black soil and fine brown soil. In some places he even made the soil red. He made squidgy clay and thick gooey mud. He made rocks of every size, from gigantic mountains to tiny grains of sand.

Then God said, 'Let the land grow every sort of grass and plant and flower and tree. Let everything have seeds inside it, so they will be able to grow again and again.'

Immediately forests of dark pine trees and orchards of trees bearing every sort of lovely fruit began to grow. Thick green grass carpeted the land and sweet-smelling meadows were filled with yellow buttercups and red poppies. He made steamy rain forests and dry sandy deserts, fields of delicious vegetables and bushes overloaded with soft fruit.

God looked at the sea and the land and all the plants and trees he had created and said, 'That is *good*!'

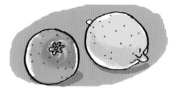

EVA'S STORY

'This is the story of what happened on the fourth day,' I told Mo.
    'Remember how I told you that God made light, so that he had both light and darkness?'
    'Yes,' said Mo.
    'Well, next he made the sun, moon and stars.'

4
Creation of the Sun and Moon

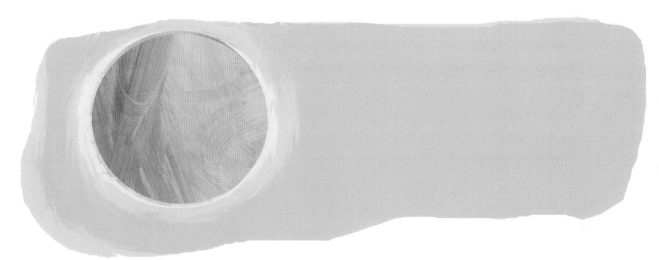

On the fourth day God decided he needed something to rule the light and the darkness and divide them up. So he created the bright golden sun to give light to the earth. He knew we would need sunlight to keep us warm and to help plants to grow.

The sun controls the seasons too, so that spring always follows winter, summer follows spring, autumn follows summer and winter follows autumn.

God also created the silver moon to shine down on us and brighten the night. Then he flung stars into space so we could see them all glittering and shining in the dark sky. God looked at the sun and moon and stars that he had made and he was pleased. He saw how beautifully they shone and said, 'That is *good*!'

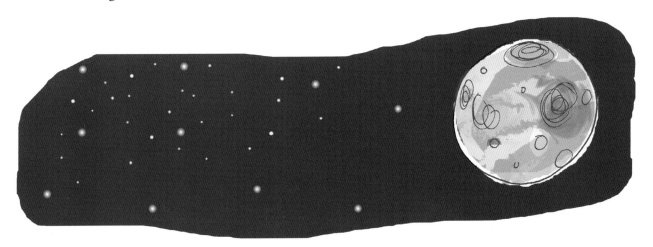

EVA'S STORY

'God made even more exciting things on the fifth day, so this is one of the stories I like best!' I said.

5
Creation of Fish and Birds

On the fifth day God looked at the sky and at the seas. Even though they were beautiful he knew there was something missing. I need some living things, he thought. So he said, 'Let there be fish in the sea!'

Suddenly the seas were full of fish and strange creatures. God made them every colour you can imagine, in thousands of strange shapes. Gigantic whales and tiny sea horses; long slithering eels and vast rays with fins like wings; spiny lobsters and scary squid. Every ocean, lake and river teemed with colourful creatures.

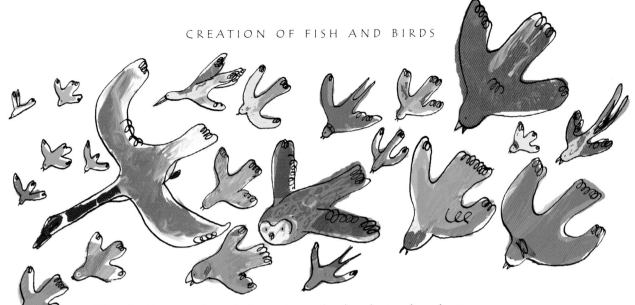

God looked up and said, 'Let there be birds in the sky!'

Immediately the skies were filled with birds of every kind and colour.

There were magnificent eagles flying over the mountains. Sea birds of all sorts swooped across the oceans. Tiny hummingbirds sipped nectar from the beautiful flowers. Huge ostriches galloped across the dry plains. Colourful parrots squawked in the steamy jungles.

God looked at the creatures he had made and he was very pleased. Then he did a very special thing. Just as he had done with the plants, he put inside each creature the seeds to make babies.

'Now my seas and my skies will always be filled with beautiful creatures,' he said. 'That is *good!*'

EVA'S STORY

'Now comes a story that's really exciting!' I told Mo. 'I'm going to tell you what happened on the sixth day. You know there's day and night, the sun, moon and stars, the sky full of birds and the seas full of fish. There's land covered with plants and trees, but nothing moved on the land. So this is what God did next.'

6
Creation of Animals

'Let there be all sorts of animals on the land!' said God, looking at his new world.

Instantly there were animals everywhere. Sheep, goats and donkeys grazed in the fields. Up in the mountains, bears climbed and leopards prowled. In the jungles were chattering monkeys and magnificent lions. Across the plains roamed tall giraffes, massive elephants with long trunks and graceful antelopes. Even the sandy deserts were full of camels, lizards and snakes. There were cats and dogs, mice and rabbits, locusts and buzzing bumblebees.

God made so many different animals it would take days to name them all. He put seeds inside each one so that forever afterwards there would be puppies and kittens, piglets and cubs and baby animals of all kinds. He looked at the animals he had made and he was very pleased.

'That is *good*!' he said.

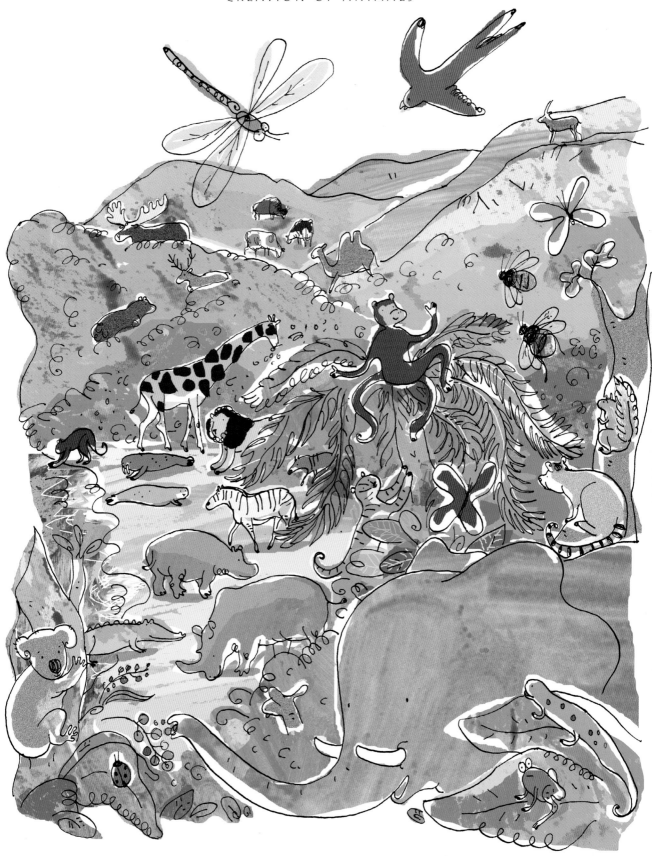

EVA'S STORY

'What happened then, Eva?' asked Mo.

'I haven't even finished the sixth day yet! The most important thing is still to come,' I said. 'God looked at everything he had made and he knew all of it was good, but there was still something missing. So he made Adam and Eve!'

'Adam and Eve had babies too, didn't they, Eva?' said Mo excitedly.

'Of course they did! Great-grandmother Eve had children and they had children and their children had children for years until Grandmother had Abba, our daddy. And he had me and named me after Eve and the last baby of all . . . was you.'

Mo thought of all those babies from Adam and Eve to himself and smiled a great big smile.

7
Creation of People

'I need someone to look after this world I have made,' said God. 'I will make people to look something like myself.'

So he took some clay and shaped it into a body and breathed life into it. It became a man who could live and breathe, walk and talk. 'I will call you *Adam*,' said God happily. 'I have made thousands of plants and animals, insects, birds and sea creatures for you. Now I want *you* to give them all names.'

So Adam named everything he saw. Although he could talk to the friendly animals, they couldn't talk back. There was nothing there like him. God knew that Adam would be lonely without somebody else, so he made a woman to be his friend and helper.

'Your name will be *Eve*', he said. 'Together you will have babies and when they grow up they will have children of their own. One day the whole earth will be full of people you have made. They may look different, because they'll be black and white, brown and yellow, but they'll all be something like me. I'm putting you two in charge of the earth and all the plants and animals I have made. You must take good care of them for me.'

God looked at the people he had made and he was very pleased. 'That is *very good*!' he said.

EVA'S STORY

'Now there's a short story for the seventh day, because God had finished making everything by then,' I said.

'Did God really make everything in just six days?' asked Mo.

'I asked Father about that. He said that God made everything before time began, so we don't know how long his days lasted. They weren't the same as our day, from getting up one morning, doing things all day, going to sleep and waking up again. His day might be as short as the time it takes you to eat a fig, or as long as millions of years! Anyway, this is what happened.'

8
The Seventh Day

The creation of the heaven and the earth was now finished. There was light and darkness; land and sea; sun, moon and stars; fish, birds and animals and even people to look after it all.

So on the seventh day God rested from his work and enjoyed looking at everything he had done. He knew that everyone would need a break from hard work and so he decided to put a rest day into his plan for his world. He blessed the seventh day and said, 'This day shall be called the *Sabbath*. It will be a holy day when my people can rest.'

EVA'S STORY

'How do you know all those things, Eva?' asked Mo.

'Grandmother has told me the stories hundreds of times,' I said. 'She heard them from her grandmother, who heard them from hers – right back to Great-Grandmother Eve.'

'Where did Eve hear them, then?' asked Mo.

'I don't know,' I replied. 'Perhaps God himself told her. Maybe when they were walking together in the Garden of Eden.'

'What's the Garden of Eden?' asked Mo.

'That's my last story,' I said.

9
The Snake in the Garden

Adam and Eve lived happily in the garden that God had made for them. It was a paradise, with lots of really friendly animals. They saw a lion cub playing with a little lamb and bears dancing with butterflies. The Garden of Eden was full of gorgeous flowers and wonderful trees, which produced the most delicious fruit imaginable.

It was warm and pleasant in the garden, so Adam and Eve didn't need to wear any clothes. They were quite happy to walk around naked and enjoy the golden sunshine and swim in the clear rivers that flowed through Eden to water the splendid plants. They could just reach out and pick lovely fruit from the trees without any effort at all. But there was a special tree in the middle of the garden that God had warned Adam about.

'This is the Tree of Knowledge', said God. 'It has the only fruit which you are forbidden to eat. If you eat it, you will die.'

Adam and Eve had so much good food from the other trees that they never thought of disobeying God and eating the forbidden fruit. Then one day a snake slithered over to talk to Eve. He was the craftiest creature God had made and he tried his hardest to get Eve into trouble.

'I'm sure you won't really die if you eat this fruit', said the snake. 'I think it will make you as clever as God himself. You will be just like him and know what is good and what is evil.'

Eve was really tempted. So she got up and picked the fruit. She ate some right away and it was so delicious that she offered it to Adam.

'Here, Adam, have a bite!' she said. 'This fruit will make us as wise as God. Surely that will be a good thing.'

Adam took the fruit and finished it off. It was good. But when he'd finished it, Adam and Eve looked at each and realised something for the first time.

'We've got no clothes on!' said Eve. 'Quick, hide behind that bush while I make us something out of those big fig leaves!'

When God came to walk in the garden that evening he found Adam and Eve still hiding behind the trees, scared to come out and see him.

'Why are you hiding?' asked God.

'We don't want you to see us because we are naked', said Adam shamefully.

'Who told you that you were naked?' asked God sternly. 'Have you eaten the forbidden fruit?'

'I did eat some', admitted Adam. 'But it was Eve's fault. She gave it to me!'

'It wasn't my fault!' said Eve. 'The snake tricked me into eating it!'

God was very angry that Adam and Eve had disobeyed him and were already bringing unhappiness and fighting into his perfect garden.

'You must leave my garden and never return', said God. 'If you had obeyed me you could have lived in this beautiful place for ever. Instead you will have to work hard to grow crops from weedy ground, full of stones and thistles, until eventually you will die.'

So God gave them animal skins to wear and sent them out of the garden for ever. He set angels with flaming swords to guard the gates of Eden. Adam and Eve knew that, because of their disobedience, they would never have such an easy, happy life again.

SHEM'S STORY

My name is Shem and my great-grandfather is a famous storyteller. He is so old now that his voice shakes when he talks, but he still tells the most amazing stories about what happened to him when he was young. His name is Shem, like mine, so perhaps I'll be a storyteller too. Or maybe a boat builder, like his father, Noah. But Noah only built a boat because God told him to.

10
Noah's Ark

People had become so wicked that God was sorry he ever made them. But Noah still loved God and obeyed him. One day God called to Noah.

'I'm going to send an enormous flood to wash away all these wicked people. So I want you to build a huge boat and save the animals.'

'But what about my family, Lord?' asked Noah. 'Please don't destroy them! And how will I build a boat big enough for *all* the animals? It's impossible!'

'Don't worry, Noah,' said God. 'You can take the whole family with you. You'll need them to help look after the animals. I'll tell you exactly how big to build the boat and guide you every step of the way. Of course you couldn't fit all the animals in! But you must take a male and a female of each kind, then they can have babies later on. Now you must start collecting wood for the boat and food for yourselves and the animals.'

So Noah got to work. He called to his sons.

'Ham, fetch me my tools, we're going to build a boat! Shem and Japheth, start cutting down trees and hauling the wood back here. Get your wives to start collecting food; we'll be making a long journey. And tar! Fetch tar to make the boat waterproof!'

So, with the help of his sons, Noah began work on the huge boat, called an ark. It took a long time to build, because it was so big. But at last it was finished. God sent a male and female of every sort of animal and Noah led them, two by two, on to the ark. Then God called Noah again.

'Get on board, Noah. In a week's time I'm going to make it rain for forty days and forty nights. But you'll be safe in the ark.'

So Noah and his wife and his sons and their wives said goodbye to the land they had lived on all their lives and climbed on board the enormous ark. Noah had all the pairs of animals aboard, plus seven pairs of all the birds. He would need these to make sacrifices to God.

The skies went black and rain poured down. The rivers and springs gushed out water from the depths of the earth until even the mountains were covered. Every bad person was drowned. But the ark floated unharmed on the raging waters.

After one hundred and fifty days God sent a wind across the waters and the floods began to disappear. The ark came to rest on the mountains of Ararat. But it was months before the waters went down enough for the trees to grow again. Noah kept sending out his birds to look for dry ground. He sent out a dove, which flew around for miles. But it could not find a dry place to land, so it returned to the ark.

Seven days later Noah sent the dove out again. When it came back to him that evening it had a fresh olive branch in its beak. A week later he sent it out again and this time it did not come back. Noah knew that it had found a dry place to roost and soon it would be safe for the animals to leave the ark.

I love to listen to my great-grandfather's stories about his life. I've often wondered what it was like for him, living with Noah and all those animals on the ark for such a long time. It's an incredible story!

11
The Rainbow Promise

Noah and his family had lived on the ark for months and months. Already, many of the animals had produced babies and it was getting very crowded. Everyone kept asking Noah when they could leave the ark.

'Just look out there,' said Noah. 'We can see lots of land now. Last week the dove came back with an olive branch in her beak. I sent her out again this morning and she hasn't come back. That must mean she's found a good place to roost. Soon it will be our turn. At least the land here will grow crops well when it dries out. We must have shovelled tons of manure overboard by now!'

But it was another twelve weeks before the ground was dry enough to live on. Then God came and spoke to Noah.

'You can leave the ark now, Noah. Release all the animals and reptiles and birds so they can go and make new homes on the dry land and raise their young.'

So Noah set all the animals free and soon the ark was empty, apart from the smell, which lingered for many months. Noah and his family climbed down the gangplank and looked at the new land God had brought them to. As Noah had guessed, it was very fertile.

'The first thing we must do is build an altar to give thanks to God for saving us from the flood,' said Noah.

So that's what they did. God was pleased with the offering they made on the altar and made this promise.

'Even though I know that there will be bad people again in the future, I will never send a flood like this to wipe out the whole world. As long as the earth remains, springtime will come and you can harvest your crops. The cold winter will follow the hot summer every year, just as day follows night. You and your family must make a new start, Noah. The world and its animals are yours, but you must look after them and use them wisely.'

'So we'll never have such terrible rain again?' asked Noah.

'Of course it will rain again!' said God. 'You need rain to make the crops grow. But if it ever rains so much that you begin to worry that I've forgotten my promise, just look up into the sky. I will put a rainbow there as a sign for you. Every time you see the beautiful colours of the rainbow shining amongst the black rain clouds, you will remember my promise.'

JAVAN'S STORY

My name is Javan and my whole family works for Abraham, a rich man with so many sheep and goats that you could never count them in one day. My father makes all the tents that Abraham and his household live in and the rest of us help him mend them when they get ripped or worn.

You get to hear everything that's going on when you're mending tents. That's how I found out that we were going on a long journey. God actually spoke to Abraham and told him to move all his family and animals to a new land.

12
Abraham's Journey

God said to Abraham, 'You must journey to Canaan. There I will make you the father of a great nation.'

Abraham was already an old man of seventy-five. He had no children, but he believed what God said. So he got his servants to round up the flocks and load everything he owned on to camels. Then he took his wife Sarah and his nephew Lot, and left. It was a long hard journey, with many stops. There was a famine and nobody had enough to eat. So Abraham took all his people to Egypt, but the Pharaoh, the ruler of Egypt, was angry with Abraham and sent them out of Egypt under armed escort.

They travelled again, until they came to the land of Canaan, where they settled down. But Lot was a rich man too and had big flocks like Abraham's. There were so many animals that there was not enough grass for them to eat. Fights began to break out between Lot's herdsmen and Abraham's as to whose animals should be allowed to graze.

Abraham knew that families shouldn't fight, so he said to Lot, 'We should split up now. You can choose which land you want first.'

So Lot looked around and thought that the fertile Jordan valley looked like the Garden of Eden. He decided to settle there, while Abraham and his servants stayed in Canaan.

JARED'S STORY

My name is Jared and my father is a brickmaker in the town of Shiloh.

'Watch me make bricks!' I said to Enoch. He's my little brother. I took the square brick mould full of squishy mud. Then I tapped it hard and the square of mud slipped out neatly. Soon I had long rows of mud bricks ready to bake dry in the hot sun. Father would be pleased with me. He has to make thousands and thousands of bricks to build new houses.

I love making bricks to build houses to make towns and cities. Yet I also know the story of how whole cities were destroyed, but a good man was saved.

13
The Wicked City

The people who lived in the cities of Sodom and Gomorrah didn't respect God and did wicked things all the time. So God decided to destroy the cities and their people. Abraham was horrified when God told him. His nephew Lot and his family lived there and he didn't want them to die.

'You're a fair and merciful God,' said Abraham. 'If you find fifty good people there, will you promise not to destroy it?'

'The people are very evil,' said God. 'But if I find fifty good people I won't destroy it.'

Then Abraham tried to bargain, in case there were not enough good people. In the end God said, 'If there are only ten good people there I will not destroy the city.'

That evening Lot saw two strangers at the city gate. He knew that the people of the city were so bad that they would do the men great harm, so he asked them home for supper.

'Don't worry about us,' said the men. 'We'll just camp out here.'

'Please come to my house and stay the night,' Lot said. 'It'll be no trouble.'

At last they agreed and went home with Lot. But after supper a big gang gathered outside Lot's house. They'd heard that he was entertaining strangers and wanted him to put them out on the street so they could ill-treat them.

Lot went out and begged them not to be so wicked. But the gang were determined to break in and get the two men. They would even have killed Lot. He and his family were in great danger.

The two men reached out, pulled Lot inside, and locked and bolted the door. The gang yelled and raged outside and were still determined to get them. But although the men looked just like ordinary men, they were really messengers sent from God. They made the gang blind for a while, so they couldn't even find the door of Lot's house and break in.

31

JAVED'S STORY

'You can put the mud into the moulds, Enoch,' I said. 'Then I'll tap it out on to the ground. If we help Father make lots of bricks he'll be able to buy a kiln. We'll build a fire inside the kiln and the bricks will dry out much quicker. Then we'll be the best brickmakers in the whole city!'

'But, Jared, what happened in the story?' asked Enoch. 'Did the wicked men get Lot?'

14
Lot's Wife

God's messengers grabbed Lot and pulled him back into his house, to save him from the angry mob. Lot was very confused 'What's happening?' he asked.

'God hasn't found even ten good men in this evil city,' said the messenger, 'so he has sent us to destroy it and every wicked person who lives here. You must hurry away with your family before it's too late!'

Lot was amazed and frightened. When dawn broke next morning, he still didn't know what to do. Would God really destroy his home and even his whole city? He knew how wicked everyone was, but it was still hard to believe.

Seeing his hesitation, the two messengers grabbed Lot and his wife and two daughters by the hands and led them from the city.

'Be quick!' they urged the family. 'Time is running out! Run towards the hills where you'll be safe! The most important thing to remember is this – don't look back!'

As the sun rose, Lot and his family fled for their lives. God rained down fire from heaven on to the cities of Sodom and Gomorrah. All the buildings and all the people were destroyed. But God saved Lot because he was a good man and had always obeyed him.

But Lot's wife did not obey God's messengers. She couldn't resist taking a last look back towards the city. And the minute she looked back she was turned into a statue made of solid salt.

ASHER'S STORY

I am Asher, a butcher's son. One day Abraham asked me to help him catch the fattest calf, and to get my father to prepare it, while Sarah his wife made some pancakes. Three guests had arrived and he wanted to give them the tenderest meat. My father always does the butchering for Abraham's tribe so I am used to helping him prepare the meat. Little did I know that one of those guests was the most important I could ever serve

15
A Son at Last

Abraham hurried to bring food to the three unexpected guests, who had seemed to appear out of nowhere. He served them roast veal and fresh pancakes as they rested under some shady trees.

'Where's Sarah your wife?' asked one of the men.

'She's in the tent,' replied Abraham, knowing that Sarah was actually listening behind the tent flap.

Now this man was really God. He told Abraham, 'When I come back here in nine months' time, Sarah will have a baby boy!'

In the tent, Sarah laughed. What a silly thing to say! She was much too old to have a baby, and Abraham was really ancient, all of a hundred years old!

Then God said to Abraham, 'Why did your wife laugh just then?

Nothing is too difficult for God. I promise you will have a son and he will be the father of nations.'

'I didn't laugh!' said Sarah, because she was embarrassed and afraid that this was really God.

But God did not hold it against her and nine months later she gave birth to a baby boy. Abraham was delighted that God had kept his promise. He named the boy Isaac, which means 'he laughs', because his wife Sarah had laughed at God's promise of a son in their old age.

OMAR'S STORY

My name is Omar and I live with my family in the Jordan valley. One day my little brother Kenan and I were watching the priest at work.

'People have brought lots of animals to the priest today,' said Kenan, watching the smoke billowing up from the fire. 'But he's not cooking them properly. They're burning up!'

'He's not cooking them, he's offering them to God,' I said. 'People bring animals or grain to the priest to burn when they want to thank God for something, or to say they are sorry for something bad that they've done.'

Then I remembered the story about how Abraham was asked to sacrifice his most treasured possession.

16
Sacrificing Isaac

Abraham really loved his son Isaac, who had grown to be a strong boy. But God decided to test Abraham's faith.

'Take Isaac up into the mountains and kill him as a sacrifice to me,' said God.

How do you think Abraham felt when he heard that? But he trusted God, so next day he got up early and chopped wood for the fire. He got two servants to stack the wood on a donkey, woke Isaac and the four of them set out on a three-day journey to the mountains.

'You two stay here,' Abraham said. 'Isaac and I will go and worship God and come back later.' So Isaac carried the wood, while Abraham carried the knife and something to start a fire.

'Where's the lamb for the sacrifice?' asked Isaac.

'God will see to that,' said Abraham.

When they reached the right place Abraham used a big flat stone for an altar. He put the wood on the altar, ready for the fire. Then he tied Isaac up and gently laid him on the wood for a sacrifice. He lifted the knife high, summoning the courage to kill his son.

Suddenly a voice called out to him from heaven, 'Abraham! Abraham! Don't hurt Isaac! You have proved that God comes first with you by being willing to sacrifice what you love most.'

Abraham heaved a great sigh of relief. He noticed a ram caught by its horns in the bushes. So he took it and sacrificed it to God in Isaac's place. Then he and Isaac and the servants went safely back home.

Abraham called the place 'God provides' and it is still called that to this day.

REBECCA'S STORY

My name is Rebecca and my father grows cucumbers and melons. I have a twin sister called Rachel and we've always been good friends, unlike some fighting twins I've heard about! While I was helping Grandmother grind the wheat for tomorrow's bread I asked her who I was named after. She told me the story of how Isaac found his wife, Rebecca, and how they had their twin boys.

17
Fighting Twins

Abraham was very old now, so he thought he'd find his son Isaac a wife. He thought the best women came from Mesopotamia, where his brother lived, so he sent his oldest servant to find a bride.

'God will help you find the right woman and bring her back here,' he told the servant.

The servant went to the city and stopped to rest his camels by a well, where the women come to get water. He prayed to God to give him a sign to show which was the right woman for Isaac.

'When I ask for a drink of water, let the right woman offer to water my camels too,' he said to God.

A beautiful young woman called Rebecca came down to the well and the servant asked her for a drink.

'Certainly, sir, you look hot and tired! And I'll give your camels a drink as well,' said Rebecca kindly.

The servant knew then that Rebecca was the right wife for Isaac. He gave her the fine ring and two gold bracelets that Abraham had sent for her and asked if he could stay with her father that night.

When they got to her house, the servant found that her father was Abraham's nephew. He told her family the story of how God had helped him find a wife for Isaac and they were happy to agree to the marriage. When the servant took Rebecca home, Isaac was delighted. He fell in love with her at once and married her immediately.

Isaac and his wife Rebecca didn't have any children for many years, then she became pregnant with twins. Even before they were born Rebecca felt as if a wrestling match was going on inside her body! God told Isaac that he planned to make the younger twin the head of the family.

The first boy was so hairy, he looked as if he was born wearing a red fur coat! They called him Esau, which means 'Hairy'. The second boy was born hanging on to his brother's foot, so they called him Jacob, which means 'Grabber'.

When the boys grew up Esau was his father's favourite because he was a good hunter, but Rebecca adored Jacob, who stayed behind quietly in the tents with his mother.

ZILPAH'S STORY

My name is Zilpah and my family are shepherds in the hills near Kedesh. One day my sister had just left to take lunch up to our brother Malachi, who was minding our sheep on the hillside. I saw she'd left something behind.

'You've forgotten the water!' I shouted, but Judith was already out of sight. It was a hot day, so I ran after her with the goatskin water bag. Judith soon came into sight and I watched as she stopped and unwrapped the fig leaves from the barley cakes I had given her.

She smelt one and I knew she was longing to eat it. Then there would only be two left for Malachi, who was always hungry! Judith sighed, wrapped up the barley cakes again and went on her way. I was so pleased that she had not cheated Malachi out of part of his dinner. He might never have found out, but it would still have been cheating. Just like the story I heard about a real cheat.

18
Jacob the Cheat

When Isaac was very old, he knew it was close to his time to die. He wanted to put his affairs in order, so he said, 'Esau, take your bow and arrows and go hunting so you can prepare a last good meal for me and I can bless you before I die.'

Rebecca heard this and said to Jacob, 'Let's trick your father into believing that you are Esau and then he'll give you his blessing to be head of the family.'

'He may be nearly blind, but he can still feel,' said Jacob. 'My skin is smooth and Esau is so hairy that he'll never believe I'm my brother!'

But Rebecca had a plan. She made Jacob put on Esau's best clothes and wrapped goatskins around his neck and arms. Then he took a delicious meal Rebecca had cooked to his father and asked for his blessing.

'Who are you?' asked his blind father.

'I'm Esau!' Jacob replied. 'I've brought that good food you asked for.'

'Come and let me feel you to make sure,' said Isaac. 'I don't think you've had time to hunt a deer *and* cook it!'

But when Jacob came close Isaac felt the hairy goatskin, smelt Esau's smell from the clothes and thought it was Esau. He gave Jacob his blessing and put him in charge of the family when he died.

When Esau came home from hunting, Isaac was shocked to find that he'd been tricked. But it was too late. Isaac could not take back the blessings he had given Jacob, even if he wanted to.

'I'm going to kill Jacob!' yelled Esau.

But Rebecca sent Jacob off to visit his uncle, where he would be safe from Esau's anger.

DEBORAH'S STORY

My name is Deborah and I live in a village beside the Sea of Galilee. Today I was with my sisters and cousins, having a sewing lesson with my grandmother.

'I hate sewing!' wailed my smallest sister as she pricked her finger for the third time. 'I'll never be any good at it!'

'All girls must learn to sew,' said Grandmother, 'otherwise we'd all have to wear animal skins like they did in olden times!'

We all giggled at the thought of that, glad of our woollen tunics, sleeveless coats and linen head cloths. But at least we could sit round in a circle together, laughing and chatting as we learnt to sew. Grandmother always told us stories and my favourite was the one about a very unusual coat, which belonged to a boy called Joseph.

19
Joseph and his Coat of Many Colours

Jacob had twelve sons, but the youngest, whose name was Joseph, was the one he loved best. Jacob gave Joseph a very special coat. It was unusual, not only because it was woven in many different colours, but because it had long sleeves. His older brothers were jealous because they hadn't been given special presents, so they hated Joseph.

Joseph worked as a shepherd with his half-brothers, and whenever they did anything wrong, he went home and told his father about it. This tale-telling made them hate Joseph even more.

Then Joseph started having dreams and was eager to tell his brothers about them.

'Last night I dreamt that we were all tying up sheaves of wheat when my sheaf stood up straight in the field and all your sheaves bowed down to mine.'

'Do you really think you're going to rule over us like that!' they asked, hating Joseph even more.

'I've had another dream!' he said, a few days later. 'I dreamt that the sun, moon and eleven stars bowed down to me!'

His brothers got very angry and even his father was cross about his boasting.

'Do you really think that your mother and I and all your brothers are going to bow down to you?' he said. But once he'd calmed down he thought about Joseph's strange dreams. He wondered if God had somehow chosen Joseph to be a leader, even though he was the youngest son. Perhaps the dreams would come true after all.

43

BUZ'S STORY

My name is Buz and I'm a camel boy. I work with my brother beside a well on the route of the traders.

'I'll ride at the head of a camel caravan one day,' I told my brother as he hauled on the rope to draw the bucket from the well. 'The long line of camels following me will be carrying exciting things from the East, colourful cloth, gum, balm and expensive myrrh. They'll all belong to me and I'll protect them from robbers with my shiny sword!'

'Take these buckets of water to the camels, Buz, or you'll never grow up to be the leader,' said my brother.

I took the water over to the camels, which had travelled so far without a drop to drink.

'Maybe I'd even find somebody exciting, like when Grandfather bought Joseph, who became such a famous man,' I said dreamily.

Joseph is Sold into Slavery

Joseph was his father's favourite son and this made all his brothers very jealous. One day the older brothers were out looking after the sheep, when Jacob called Joseph to him.

'Your brothers are all in the fields with the sheep, Joseph,' said Jacob. 'Go and see what they're up to for me.'

So Joseph set out, but his brothers saw him coming.

'Let's kill that awful Joseph, and throw his body down a well!' said Levi. 'We'll tell Father he was eaten by a lion!' said Judah.

'Don't kill him, put him down an empty well to starve', said Reuben, the eldest, who was just leaving. He secretly planned to come back and rescue Joseph.

As soon as Joseph arrived, his brothers took his fine coat of many colours, then threw him down a well. They sat down to eat, ignoring his cries for help. Soon, a long line of camels came by. It was traders on their way to Egypt.

'Let's sell Joseph to those traders', said Judah. 'Then we'll get some money as well as getting rid of that annoying dreamer!'

So they pulled Joseph out of the well and sold him for twenty silver coins. When Reuben came back and found the well empty, he was very upset. The brothers had covered up what they had done by tearing Joseph's coat and dipping it in goat's blood. They took it back home and showed their father.

'Oh no!' cried Jacob. 'That's Joseph's coat! He must have been attacked and eaten by a wild animal!'

Nobody could comfort Jacob, for he had lost his favourite son. He did not know that Joseph was now a slave in the household of the king of Egypt.

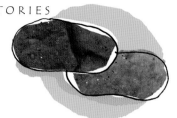

IRA'S STORY

I'm Ira and I work in a baker's shop in Hebron. I'm glad my job isn't grinding flour. It's hard work, and I'd be scared of getting my fingers caught between the stones. It's so dusty too! Someone sieves the flour, then passes it on to the next boy, who mixes it with water and yeast to make dough. The baker always likes to do the next bit himself, because he says it's the most important. He kneads the dough, then shapes it into round loaves.

My job comes next. I take the bread stamp by its handle and press it into each loaf in turn. It's the easiest job in the bakery, even though the wooden stamp is quite heavy. While I'm stamping the loaves, ready for the oven, the baker likes me to repeat the tales my mother tells me at home. His favourite one has a bit about the king of Egypt's baker, who came to a nasty end.

21
Joseph and the Pharaoh

Joseph's brothers were so jealous of him that they sold him to some slave traders on their way to Egypt. When the traders reached Egypt, they sold Joseph into the household of the Pharaoh, who was Egypt's king. At first he did very well but then his master's wife had him put into prison. Here he met Pharaoh's wine steward and chief baker. They'd both made Pharaoh angry, so he'd locked them up.

One night, both men had very strange dreams. Joseph told the wine steward, 'Your dream about squeezing the juice from grapes on three branches into the Pharaoh's cup means that in three days you'll get your job back.'

'What about my dream?' the baker asked eagerly. 'I dreamt that I was carrying three boxes of cakes on my head, but birds were eating the pastries in the top box.'

'I'm afraid it's bad news,' said Joseph sadly. 'Your dream means that in three days Pharaoh will have you killed and throw your body to the birds to eat.'

It happened exactly as Joseph had said. Two years later, the Pharaoh himself had a strange dream. The wine steward told him about Joseph, so Pharaoh asked him to explain the dream.

'Only God knows the meaning of dreams,' said Joseph. 'Tell me about it and God will help me explain.'

Pharaoh told him about seven thin cows who ate seven fat cows and seven ripe ears of corn, which were swallowed up by seven, thin scrawny ones. God gave Joseph the explanation.

'God is telling you that after seven good years there will be seven bad years of famine, when no crops will grow,' said Joseph. 'You must save food wisely so your people will have enough to eat.'

Pharaoh thought Joseph was so clever that he put him in charge. For seven years, the crops grew well. Joseph travelled around the country, collecting the extra grain and storing it safely. When the famine came there was enough food to give to the starving people of Egypt.

There was no food in Canaan either, so Jacob sent his sons to Egypt to find some. Joseph forgave his brothers and used his power to help his family, even though they had sold him into slavery.

MIRIAM'S STORY

My name is Miriam and all my family weave baskets. My ancestors used to live in Egypt, which was a very scary thing at the time, because they were all slaves. The one I like to hear and tell about most is Miriam. It's partly because we share the same name and are both good at weaving baskets. But it's mostly because her quick thinking saved the family from losing her baby brother when he was tiny.

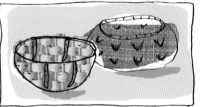

22
The Baby in the Bulrushes

Pharaoh was frightened of the Israelites. Even though he had made them slaves, he was worried because there were so many of them. 'Send for all the women who help the Israelite women have their babies!' he roared.

When all the midwives came he gave them an order.

'Every time a Hebrew woman has a boy baby you are to kill it!'

But the midwives feared God more than the Pharaoh and let the new baby boys live, even though Pharaoh wanted them thrown into the river to feed the huge crocodiles that lived there.

One Hebrew woman had a lovely baby boy. She managed to keep him hidden until he was three months old, but then he grew so strong and cried so vigorously that she could hide him no longer.

'Go and gather some papyrus reeds from the river, Miriam,' said the mother to her daughter. 'Then you can help me weave a strong basket.'

They made the basket, then the mother gently laid her baby boy inside and pushed it out into the river Nile.

'Watch out for him, Miriam!' she said, with tears in her eyes. 'Make sure no crocodiles get him!'

Miriam ran along the bank, keeping close watch on the basket. When she heard voices she hid in the reeds. Pharaoh's daughter had come down to the river and heard the baby's sudden cry.

'It's a poor little Hebrew baby!' she said, as her servants took the baby out and unwrapped him for her to see. 'I'd like to look after him, but he's so tiny!'

Miriam bravely went up to the princess and said, 'Shall I go and fetch a Hebrew woman who can feed the baby and look after him for you while he is so little?'

The princess agreed and Miriam ran to fetch her mother.

'Look after this baby and I will pay you well!' said the princess. 'I'll call him Moses, because that means "drawn out of the water".'

So Moses had his own mother to care for him and a clever older sister to play with him.

MIRIAM'S STORY

Reeds and grasses can be woven into all sorts of things. I have only learned to make mats and baskets so far. But my parents make really difficult things. Sandals are hard to weave, but of course everyone needs them to protect their feet from the stony ground, so they make lots of them.

Moses had to take his sandals off when he met God in the burning bush, because it was holy ground. I wonder if he had sandals like the ones my mother weaves?

23
The Burning Bush

Moses left Egypt when he was grown-up, and became a shepherd. One day he was looking after his sheep when he saw a bush on fire. He went closer to warm himself and was amazed to see that although there were lots of flames the bush wasn't burning away.

Suddenly the voice of God called out from inside the bush, 'Don't come any closer, Moses! This is holy ground. Take your sandals off! I am the God of Abraham, Isaac and Jacob!'

Moses hid his face, for he was afraid to look at God.

'I have heard the cries of my people suffering in slavery in Egypt,' said God, 'and I've chosen you to go to Pharaoh and tell him to let them go!'

'Why choose me?' asked Moses in alarm. 'Nobody will believe that God has sent me. If I say I've seen you, they'll just call me a liar!'

'Throw your rod upon the ground!' said God.

Moses threw down the big stick and instantly God turned it into a writhing snake. Moses ran away as quickly as he could.

'Come back and pick it up by the tail,' said God.

Nervously Moses picked up the snake, which turned back into a rod again. God gave Moses other signs to prove to the people that he had seen God, but still Moses made excuses.

'I won't know what to say!' he pleaded. 'Please send someone else!'

'Don't you trust me to tell you what to say?' said God angrily. 'Your brother Aaron is a good speaker. You will go to Egypt together and he can do the talking.'

So Moses set out on his difficult task.

JAKE'S STORY

I'm Jake and my father owns a vineyard. The job in my father's vineyard that I love watching best is treading the grapes. I help pour the baskets of grapes into the big stone winepress, then the men jump into the winepress and squash the grapes with their bare feet. I'd love to do it too, but I'm not tall enough yet.

'It will be a few years yet before you can reach up to hold on to the ropes hanging from the wooden beam, Jake,' says my father.

Suddenly hail pelts down from the grey sky. We run for shelter and watch the hard cold hail rain down on the vineyard.

'This won't do my vines any good at all,' says Father gloomily. 'I'd say it was the worst hail I've ever seen!'

As I watched the hailstones rain down I thought about the hailstones and other plagues sent to Egypt.

24
The Plagues of Egypt

Moses and Aaron had been given a task by God. They journeyed to Egypt to see the Pharaoh and give him God's message. 'God doesn't want the Israelites to be slaves', they told him. 'You must let my people go!'

But Pharaoh wouldn't let them go. He was so angry that he made them work even harder. So God told Moses to go back to Pharaoh and ask him again. Aaron threw down his rod before the king and it became a hissing snake.

'My magicians can do just as well!' said the king, and wouldn't listen to Moses.

God made the River Nile turn from water into blood. The fish all died and nobody could drink. But Pharaoh still wouldn't let the Israelites go.

Then God sent a plague of frogs. Everywhere you looked there were thousands of frogs! There were frogs in people's beds, in their ovens and in their food.

'Get rid of the frogs and I'll let the Israelites go!' promised Pharaoh.

Moses asked God to remove the frogs, but Pharaoh broke his promise and still wouldn't let the people go.

So God sent millions of gnats upon the land. Soon every man and beast was covered in nasty, biting insects.

'I'm still not letting them go!' said Pharaoh stubbornly.

God sent another plague. Swarms of flies covered everything. They crawled all over people's faces and covered their food like a blanket. Only the Israelites had no flies near them. It was so bad that Pharaoh again agreed to let the people go if God removed the flies.

But when all the flies were gone, Pharaoh broke his promise again. This time God sent a plague that killed all the Egyptians' cattle and other animals. Still Pharaoh was stubborn.

'I'm not letting a single one go!' he said.

God told Moses to take lots of ashes and throw them up into the air. Wherever the ashes landed a nasty painful sore came on the Egyptians and their animals. Even the magicians had sores all over them. But Pharaoh wouldn't change his mind.

Then the heaviest hail that the Egyptians had ever seen fell upon them. It was so bad that every man and animal outside was killed and every tree and plant flattened.

'The flax and the barley are ruined!' said Pharaoh. 'Tell your God to stop the hail before the wheat comes up and I'll let your people go!'

Moses asked God to stop the hail, but still Pharaoh refused to release the slaves. So God sent so many locusts that the skies were black with them. These enormous hungry insects ate up every plant and fruit still in Egypt, so there was nothing left to eat.

'Ask your God to forgive me and take the locusts away and I'll do what you want!' promised Pharaoh.

But, yet again, he broke his promise. God sent darkness on the land so it was pitch black for three days and nights and nobody could leave their homes.

'Get away from me with your plagues!' said Pharaoh to Moses. 'I never want to see you or your people again!'

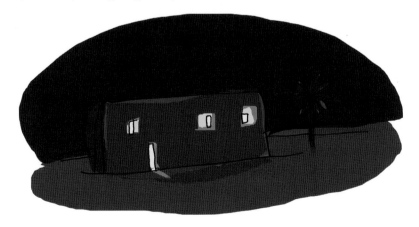

JAKE'S STORY

Once the hailstorm was over, Father and I went to inspect the vines.

'The vines are a bit battered but the grapes seem to be fine, Jake,' said Father.

'Even losing the whole crop wouldn't be as bad as what happened to the Egyptians when their stubborn king wouldn't keep his promise,' I said.

25
Death Passes Over

God had sent terrible plagues over Egypt, but no matter what happened, Pharaoh refused to release the Israelites from slavery in his country. Before Moses had seen Pharaoh for the last time, God told him that he was going to send one more plague. Moses told Pharaoh about it before he left.

'God will pass through Egypt at midnight and every first-born male will be killed. The air will be filled with the cries and tears of sorrowful parents. Only the Hebrew people will be spared. Then you will come and *beg* me to take my people and leave!'

Moses angrily left Pharaoh and went back to his people to tell them what to do so they could be safe when death came to Egypt.

'Every family is to choose a fine lamb and kill it this evening,' he said. 'Then use its blood to paint along the doorposts outside your house. Nobody must leave their house tonight! Stay safely indoors and keep the door tightly shut while God passes through the land. When he sees the blood he will pass over your houses and not let anything hurt you.

'You must eat the lamb roasted; have your coats and sandals on, so you are ready to leave. Then you must remember this Passover by doing the same thing every year to remind yourselves and your children how God spared his people while the Egyptians were killed.'

So the people did exactly as Moses had told them. That night every Egyptian household lost their eldest son, as well as the first born of all the animals. But the Hebrew people stayed safe. Pharaoh sent messengers to Moses and begged him to leave.

In the early morning light the Hebrew slaves left Egypt at last. Six hundred thousand men took their families and their flocks and all their possessions and set off into the desert. They were free at last.

KOZ'S STORY

My name is Koz and I am the son of a fisherman on the Sea of Galilee. I spend hours and hours on the fishing boat with my father. I often wonder what's down at the bottom of the sea. The Israelites saw the bottom of the Red Sea when Moses parted the waves to let them cross safely. The Egyptians would have seen it too. But they never got to tell anyone about it, because they were washed away and drowned!

26
Parting the Red Sea

God led the Israelites through the wilderness towards the Red Sea. He went with them in a pillar of cloud in the daytime and a pillar of flames at night. These pillars moved ahead of them so that they always knew which way to go.

Back in Egypt, Pharaoh was very angry at the loss of all his slaves.

'I need those Hebrews to work for me!' he said. 'Get the whole army ready! We'll capture them and bring them back!'

So the Egyptian army set off to chase after the Israelites, who were camped by the water. When they saw the huge cloud of dust raised by more than six hundred chariots, the Israelites knew that Pharaoh was after them. They were terrified and turned to Moses in anger.

'Why did you bring us out here?' they wailed. 'It would have been better to stay and live as slaves than to be killed out here in this awful desert!'

'Don't be frightened,' said Moses. 'God will save us all and destroy the Egyptian army!'

'Point your rod over the sea,' said God to Moses. 'I will push back the sea so that my people can cross in safety.'

So Moses held his big staff out over the raging sea. Immediately the water was divided by a strong east wind, leaving a dry path down the middle for the people to cross. The huge pillar of cloud went behind them now, so that the Egyptians couldn't see them.

But soon the Egyptian army found the dry path and followed them, getting closer every minute. By the time the last of the Israelites had safely crossed the sea, the fast horses of the Egyptian chariots had almost caught up with them.

God told Moses to raise his rod over the sea once more. As he did so, the huge walls of water tumbled down upon the charging Egyptians like a giant tidal wave. Every single one of them was drowned.

Moses and his people were so thankful to be saved that they sang joyfully and danced in celebration, before setting out on their journey once more.

MARA'S STORY

My name is Mara and I help my mother make butter. First I heat milk in a pottery churn. Then I add sour goat's milk and stir vigorously. Butter making is hard work but I always think how good the bread and butter will taste when it's made. It reminds me of a story about the days when the Israelites didn't have anything to eat, so God sent food from heaven

27
Food from Heaven

God rescued the fleeing Israelites by parting the Red Sea so they could cross. Although they were now safe from the Egyptian army their struggles were far from over. After a few weeks in the desert the Israelites started complaining to Moses.

'At least we had enough to eat in Egypt! Why did you bring us here to starve?'

'God will look after you even though you complain so much,' said Moses. 'God will send us food from heaven. There will be meat to eat tonight, and tomorrow we will find bread.'

Later that evening, thousands of quails flew down. The people caught the little birds, cooked them and ate until they were full. Next morning the Israelites found a special food called 'manna' on the ground. The people had never seen the white flakes before and didn't know what they were.

'Eat it, it's delicious!' said Moses. 'But don't gather more than you need for today or it will go rotten. Only on the day before the Sabbath can you gather twice as much, so you won't have to work that day.'

All the time the Israelites were in the desert God sent them quails and manna every day, so they never went hungry. But sometimes there was no water to drink and the people got angry with Moses again.

God told him to hit a big rock with his staff. When Moses did so, water gushed from the rock like a stream. So, despite their complaints, God made sure that his people always had enough food and drink.

LEVI'S STORY

I am Levi, a donkey boy, and I work for Balaam, who is an important man, a prophet. Even the king listens to him, because God speaks directly to Balaam. My favourite donkey is called Judy and I'd just brought food for her.

'Here's some fresh hay, Judy,' I said. 'How are you feeling today?'

I listened hard, but the donkey made no reply. I sighed. I'd been trying to encourage her to talk to me for months but I'd not heard a single word since the day my master told me to saddle up Judy to take him to visit King Balak. The king wanted Balaam to ask God to send great evil to hurt the Israelites. But God used an amazing miracle to show Balaam what to do.

The Amazing ²⁸Talking Donkey

The Israelites camped near the land of King Balak, in Moab. Balak was terrified that such a huge number of Israelites would take over his land so he asked Balaam to curse them. Balaam asked God about it many times, but God always told him not to do it.

But Balaam loved money, so he was excited when at last God said to him, 'Go then, but say exactly what I tell you.' They were riding along, when suddenly his donkey stood still. She could see an angel holding a sword in front of them. Frightened, she turned off into a field.

As Balaam hit the donkey and pulled her back on to the road, the angel moved further down. When the donkey tried to squirm past the angel by pressing hard against the wall, Balaam's foot got crushed against the hard stones. He roared with rage, beating her hard.

They came to a narrow place where they couldn't pass the angel, so Balaam's donkey lay down in the road. He was furious and beat her even harder.

Then God made the animal talk like a person.

'Why have you beaten me three times?'

Furiously, Balaam replied, 'You're making a fool of me! I should kill you!'

'Do I usually behave like this?' asked the donkey.

'Well . . . no', admitted Balaam.

Then God opened Balaam's eyes to what the donkey had seen all along. Balaam fell down on his knees before the angel standing in the road with his drawn sword.

'Why have you beaten your donkey three times?' asked the angel. 'If she hadn't got out of my way I would have killed you with my sword and saved her life.'

'Forgive me! I was greedy for money', moaned Balaam. 'Shall I go home now?'

'No, go to King Balak. But say only what God tells you', said the angel.

When Balaam met King Balak, he refused to curse the Israelites. Three times, King Balak tried to persuade Balaam, offering him more and more rewards. But Balaam blessed them instead. King Balak was very angry.

'I could make you rich, but your God has kept you from that! Get out of here! I never want to see you again!'

So Balaam and his donkey returned home safely.

TAMAR'S STORY

My name is Tamar and I'm the daughter of a flax spinner. There is a lot of work to do before the flax is ready for spinning and my sisters and I try to help. Mother put down the large wooden club she used for pounding the wet flax and rubbed her sore back. It was hard work separating the fibres from the stalk.

'I've already taken down the dry flax from the roof,' she said. 'I'll start spinning that now and soon there'll be a big batch to take to the weavers. Now, please will you girls take all this flax up on to the roof and spread it to dry?'

My sisters and I climbed up with our bundles of soggy flax. As we spread out the wet fibres on our big flat roof I remembered a story about someone who hid something dangerous under the flax on her roof.

29
Rahab and the Spies

Moses lived to be very old and after he died God made Joshua the leader of the Israelites. Joshua sent two men to spy out the Promised Land. The spies went to the city of Jericho and stayed at the house of a woman called Rahab. But the king heard about the Hebrew spies and sent soldiers to Rahab's house to capture them.

'Two men were here earlier,' said Rahab, when the soldiers came. 'But they've left now. You'd better chase them quickly, or you won't be able to catch them!'

When the soldiers had left she climbed up on to her flat roof where drying flax was laid out in neat rows.

'You can come out now,' she whispered. 'The soldiers have gone.'

The two spies crawled out from under the flax.

'The whole country is scared of you Israelites,' said Rahab. 'We heard how your God even parted the Red Sea for you when you came out of Egypt. He must be a very great God! Promise me that you will not kill my family when you take over our city!'

'Don't worry,' said the spies. 'You saved us, so we'll save you. Bring all your relatives here to stay. Then hang a scarlet cord from the window so our men know not to attack your house.'

It was late and the gates of the city had been locked, so the spies couldn't walk out. But Rahab's house was built into the city wall. So they climbed down a rope from her window and escaped safely.

JESSE'S STORY

I am called Jesse and my father makes trumpets for the priests. He is very pleased today because he has two new sons, but my brother Sol and I are not so sure.

'What an awful noise!' grumbled Sol, and put his fingers in his ears. I did the same, but it didn't help much. We could still hear our new twins screaming their heads off.

'You and Jesse were just as bad when you were babies,' said Father, as he polished a ram's horn to make it into a trumpet. 'The whole family would have made good members of Joshua's army!'

'Whose army?' asked Sol.

'Joshua's army used horns like this to capture a city,' I explained. 'The priests made them into trumpets called *shofars*.'

30
Walls Come Tumbling Down

Joshua and his army had surrounded the city of Jericho, ready to capture it. God told Joshua what to do.

'Every day for the next seven days I want you to march your army round the city. Behind the soldiers put seven priests carrying trumpets. At the end of the week you will all march round seven times with the priests blowing on their *shofars*. At the last blast from the trumpets I want all the army to shout as loudly as they can. Then the walls of the city will collapse and you can capture it easily.'

Joshua told the army exactly what to do. For six days they all marched silently round the city. The people of Jericho watched this strange procession in disbelief. They wondered how Joshua's army could possibly capture their city this way, but they did not know about God's promise.

Then on the seventh day Joshua said, 'God will give us this city if we shout with all our strength. Remember not to kill Rahab and her family in the house with the scarlet cord hanging from the window. Do not steal anything for yourselves, but bring everything valuable you capture back to me for God's treasury.'

So for the seventh time the army marched round the city, the trumpets sounded, and the men yelled with all their might. The walls of Jericho came tumbling down and it was easy for the army to leap over all the rubble and capture the city. But they spared Rahab, who had believed that their God was the true god.

The Israelites had begun to capture the Promised Land.

JESSE'S STORY

My father makes fine trumpets and when I grow up I'd like to play one of his trumpets in a battle, like the priests used to do. I know another good story about trumpets in battle.

31
Gideon Puts Out a Fleece

After Joshua died the Israelites were without a leader. Midian was the land east of the Red Sea and for seven years the Midianites ruled the Israelites. They stole their grain and animals so the Israelites had to hide in caves to escape them. An angel came to a man called Gideon with a message from God.

'I have chosen you to save Israel', said God. 'You will be a mighty warrior.'

Gideon was shocked. 'My tribe is the smallest', he said, 'and I'm the least important person in it! Why pick me?'

'With you as leader, the Israelites will defeat the Midianites', promised God.

Gideon called all the other tribes to help him in the battle. But he was still worried, so he prayed to God.

'I'll put out a woollen fleece tonight', Gideon said. 'If the fleece is wet tomorrow morning and the floor around it is dry, I'll know you mean what you say.'

Next morning the fleece was soaking wet and the floor dry, but Gideon was still nervous.

'I'll put out the fleece again tonight, Lord. If it stays dry while the floor becomes wet, I'll know for *sure* that you want me to save Israel.'

Sure enough, the fleece stayed dry, so Gideon prepared for battle.

Gideon had more than thirty thousand men ready when God said to him, 'With this many men they will think it is their own bravery that makes you win, not the help of God. Send most of them home!'

So Gideon was left with only three hundred men to fight against the huge Midianite army. He gave each man a torch, a jar and a trumpet. The men carried the burning torches in the pottery jars, so their enemies couldn't see the flames.

'Creep up on our enemies silently while they are sleeping,' ordered Gideon. 'When I give the word, smash the jars and wave your flaming torches, blow your trumpets and yell, "For the Lord and Gideon!" and we'll be sure to win!'

When the Midianites woke up and heard the shrieking of the *shofars*, and the yells of the men and saw the flaming torches they panicked, because they thought they were surrounded. They ran away, even attacking each other in their confusion. Gideon and his small band of Israelites had won the battle with the help of God.

TIMNA'S STORY

I'm Timna, and my mother is a sweet maker in the town of Nain. I love watching her making the delicious sweets, but I love eating them even more.

'I'm ready to add the honey to the cakes now,' said Mother.

'I'll get it!' I said, carefully carrying the heavy pot across the room.

'You must be as strong as Samson to carry that heavy pot!' Mother said admiringly.

As she poured in the pure syrup I remembered the amazing story of Samson, the strong man.

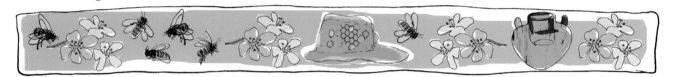

32
Samson and Delilah

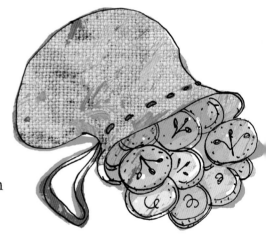

When Samson was born, God told his parents that his hair must never be cut because he would be a special man, who would help the Israelites against their enemies, the Philistines.

Samson grew up to be so strong that one day he ripped a wild lion apart with his bare hands. He killed a thousand of his enemies with the jawbone of an ass. This made the Philistines terrified of him.

Then he fell in love with a woman called Delilah. The Philistines offered to pay Delilah eleven hundred pieces of silver if she would find out the secret of Samson's strength.

'You are so strong!' she said to Samson. 'How could anyone overpower you?'

Samson told her that being tied up with fresh bowstrings would take away his strength. Then he told her that tying him up with new ropes or plaiting his hair would take away his strength. But each time Samson broke free easily.

Delilah kept pestering Samson to tell her his secret, but each time he fooled her.

'Why won't you tell me the secret of your strength?' cried Delilah. 'If you *really* loved me you wouldn't tease me like this!'

So Samson told her the secret.

Immediately Delilah told the Philistines and that night they crept in and shaved off all Samson's hair while he was asleep. When Delilah woke him up he could not fight the Philistines because his hair had kept him strong and now it was gone. He was captured, blinded and put in prison.

Much later, the Philistine rulers were having a feast with thousands of people in their temple. They remembered Samson and had him brought out of prison to entertain them.

Samson prayed to God.

'Make me strong again so I can kill these Philistines who blinded me. Then I will die happy.'

Samson's hair had grown long again while he was in prison. He was standing between two stone pillars, which he pushed apart with his strong arms. They crashed to the floor, bringing the roof falling down and killing everyone in the temple, including Samson. He killed more of his enemies with this one act than he had in the whole of his life.

SARAH'S STORY

My name is Sarah and my father is a farmer in the Jordan valley. My father always leaves a strip of barley unharvested at the edge of his fields. It is the law and it is also the only way that poor people like widows and orphans can find any food to eat. I know a story about a widow called Naomi.

33
Ruth and Naomi

Naomi was an Israelite, but she lived in Moab with her husband, her two sons and their wives. When her husband and sons died she decided to travel back to her home village of Bethlehem. But Ruth, one of her daughters-in-law, loved her dearly and didn't want to leave her.

'I will come with you,' said Ruth. 'Your land will be my land and your God will be my God.'

So they went to
Bethlehem, but as
they didn't have any
way of getting food
Ruth went to glean in
the fields of Boaz, a relative
of Naomi. She was picking
up leftover grain for them to eat
when Boaz found out who she was. He
told her to stay with his servants and take as
much grain as she wanted.

'Why are you so kind to me?' she asked.

'I've been told how good you've been to Naomi,' he said. 'You left your
own country and came here to live with foreigners, just to look after her.'

Naomi was thrilled when she heard that Ruth had got on so well with
Boaz. She told Ruth to put on her best clothes and go to visit
Boaz at night. Ruth went and lay at his feet as he slept.

When he woke up he said, 'I'd
like to marry you, Ruth. By law the
wedding will be allowed if I can
buy the field that belonged to
Naomi's husband.'

So Boaz arranged to
buy the field and soon he
and Ruth were happily
married. Naomi was so
thrilled when a little
grandson was born,
that she praised God
for his goodness.

LEAH'S STORY

My name is Leah and my family keeps goats to make cheese that we sell in the market-place. I'm the oldest girl in the family so I help by looking after the little ones. There always seem to be a couple of toddlers in our house and I enjoy playing with them. But what I really love is to hold a new baby in my arms and rock it to sleep. It must be so sad not to have any children at all! I hope I have lots when I grow up. I know a story about someone who wanted a baby very badly.

34
Hannah Keeps her Promise

Hannah longed for children of her own. Her husband Elkanah had another wife, Peninnah, as was the custom in their country, and they had children. Peninnah was horrible to Hannah and always made fun of her.

Every year they journeyed to the temple at Shiloh, to worship and make sacrifices to God. Peninnah teased Hannah all the way, making her cry so much she couldn't eat. Elkanah tried to cheer her up, because he really loved Hannah, but she was not comforted.

One evening Hannah returned to the temple and wept bitterly as she prayed silently to God.

'Please, God, if you will give me a son, I promise I'll let him serve in your temple for the whole of his life.'

Hannah's lips moved silently as she prayed. Eli, the priest, saw this and thought she was drunk. He was very angry.

'You cannot come to God's house in a drunken state!' he shouted.

'I'm not drunk!' said Hannah. 'I'm just so very sad. I was telling God my troubles and asking him to help me.'

'In that case, may God grant your wish,' replied the priest.

Hannah was filled with hope at Eli's words. In time, God answered her prayers and gave her a fine son.

'I asked God for him, so I'll call him Samuel,' she said happily, 'because Samuel means "asked of God".'

When Samuel was big enough to eat proper food and run about the house, Hannah took him back to the temple.

'Do you remember me?' she asked Eli. 'A few years ago you saw me praying silently to God. He has answered my prayer and given me this beautiful son, Samuel. Now I want to fulfil my promise. I am giving my son back to God, so that he may serve him in the temple all his life.'

Eli praised God for Hannah's faithfulness and took Samuel in to learn to help in the temple. Every year Hannah visited Samuel and brought a new little coat that she had sewn especially for him.

ABIMELECH'S STORY

My name's Abimelech, but my friend Samuel calls me Bim. I've just come here to work in the temple, which is God's house, where people come to worship him. Samuel's been working with Eli, the chief priest, since he was a tiny boy. Samuel's just told me the weirdest story, so I'll tell you and see if you think God's got a special job ahead for him

35
The Voice in the Night

Poor old Eli the priest is nearly blind now. His sons are really evil men and don't love or serve God. Samuel was sleeping, but woke up when he heard someone calling him. He knew it must be Eli, so he ran down to his room.

'Here I am!' Samuel yawned. 'What do you want?'

'Nothing, Samuel!' said Eli. 'I never called you!'

Three times he heard the call, but he wasn't wanted.

The third time Samuel said, 'I definitely heard you calling my name, Eli!'

Eli sat up in bed and got very excited.

'Messages from God are very rare in these sad times, Samuel,' he said. 'But I'm sure it's him calling your name! He must have an important message for us!

'Go back to bed. If he calls your name, you must say, "Speak, Lord. Your servant is listening." '

Samuel went slowly back to bed. Why should God choose a small boy like him to talk to? A few minutes later he heard God call.

'Samuel! Samuel!'

'Speak, Lord. Your servant is listening,' he whispered, very scared.

'I have warned Eli that I would judge his whole family if he didn't stop his sons behaving in the wicked way they do. But he has done nothing to stop them, so I have decided they will all be punished.'

It was an important message from God to Eli. But why tell Samuel, who was too scared to say anything? He pulled the bedcovers over his head and stayed there, shivering, until morning. But then he had to get up and open the doors of the temple so the people could get in to worship. He rushed round the temple, doing his jobs and trying to avoid Eli. But it wasn't long before Eli caught up with Samuel.

'Tell me exactly what God said to you last night!'

So Samuel had to tell him about God's punishment. Eli sighed deeply and said, 'He is God. He must do what he thinks is right. God is blessing your work here, Samuel. I think he wants you to be a prophet, a man who speaks God's words to his people.'

JOEL'S STORY

My name is Joel and I'm the son of an olive grower. One day when I was walking through my father's olive grove I heard the sound of loud crying. It was a boy, his fists pressed into his eyes and tears pouring down his cheeks.

'Whatever's the matter?' I asked.

'My donkey run away!' he wailed.

'I'll help you find him,' I said.

As we searched for the donkey I remembered a story I'd heard. It was about a handsome young man, taller than anyone else, who heard some amazing news while he was looking for his lost donkeys.

36
Saul for King

Samuel was a good man and the people listened to him. When he was old he made his sons judges, but they were bad men and the people didn't want them.

'We want a king like all the other countries!' they said.

'A king will make you obey him and give him most of your possessions,' warned Samuel. 'Then you'll wish you'd never asked for one.'

But the people insisted, so Samuel asked God to help him choose a king. Next day Samuel met a young man called Saul.

'I've been searching for my donkeys for three days,' said Saul. 'They say you are a man of God. Can you tell me where they are?'

'Your donkeys have been found,' said Samuel. 'Come and eat with me and I will tell you what God has chosen for you.'

After their meal Samuel poured some holy oil on Saul's head to show that God had a special job for him to do.

'God has chosen you to be king,' said Samuel. 'I've called all the Israelites together next week. Make sure you come to the meeting so that I can tell them about you.'

But when the time came for the meeting, Saul was nowhere to be seen. He was so scared of being chosen king that he had hidden among the tents and baggage that all the people had brought. But someone found him and brought him out to show the people.

'Here is your king!' said Samuel.

The people saw how tall and handsome Saul was and began to shout and cheer. 'Long live the king!' they shouted.

JOEL'S STORY

We found the lost donkey trying to nibble the leaves of one of the young olive trees.

'Don't eat that!' I yelled, grabbing the donkey's rope and pulling it away from the tree. 'That's my tree! My father planted it for me when I was born.'

'It's not a very good tree,' said the boy. 'It doesn't even have any olives!'

'Olive trees don't have any fruit for the first fifteen years,' I said. 'But they will be the best olives in the world. The priests mix the olive oil with cinnamon, cassia and myrrh to make a special anointing oil that they use to anoint a new king.'

37
From Shepherd Boy to King

Saul was king for a long time, but he disobeyed God, who decided to choose a new king. Samuel was upset about this, but God said to him, 'Fill up your ram's horn with anointing oil and go to Bethlehem. I'm going to make one of Jesse's sons king.'

So Samuel went to Bethlehem, where Jesse lived, and asked to see his sons. The eldest son, Eliab, was big and strong and Samuel thought that he must be the one God had chosen. But God said to him, 'I am not like ordinary people who only look at the outside of a person. What they are like inside is much more important. That's what I look at!'

Samuel looked at all seven of Jesse's sons, who were all fine men, but Samuel knew that none of them was God's chosen king.

'Do you have any other sons?' he asked.

'Only my youngest boy, David,' said Jesse. 'He's out looking after the sheep.'

Samuel asked Jesse to fetch David. When he came in, Samuel saw he was strong and bright-eyed.

'This is the one,' God said to Samuel. 'Anoint David with oil. I have chosen him to be the new King of Israel.'

So Samuel poured the holy oil on the shepherd boy and David was filled with the Holy Spirit.

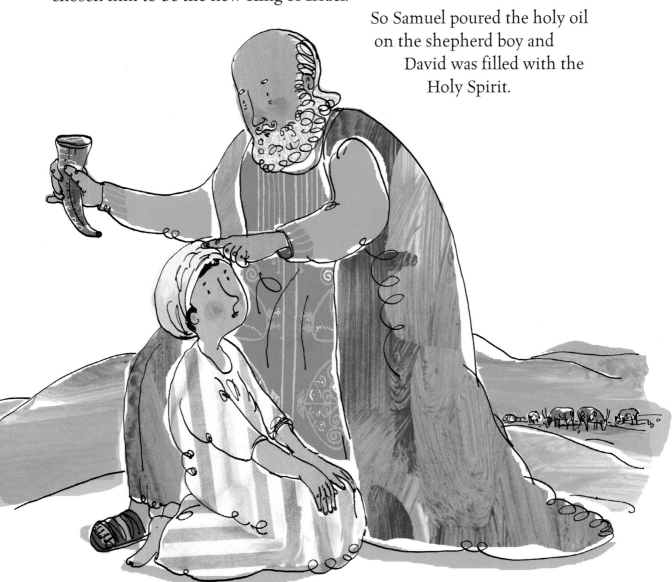

MILCAH'S STORY

My name is Milcah and my brother is a shepherd boy. Tonight will be the first night he's spent with the flock out on the hills. He's watching me impatiently as I make him a new sling. He'll need it in case lions or bears come and try to steal the sheep.

'Don't worry about tonight, Jemuel!' I said, as I finished sewing. 'This is a very strong sling and you're a good shot, like another shepherd boy called David.'

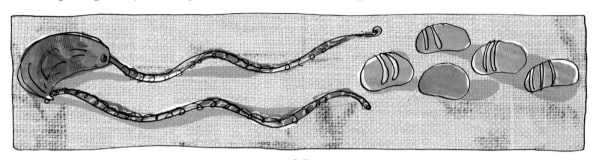

38
David and Goliath

The armies of Israel and their enemies, the Philistines, were at war. For forty days Goliath, the biggest man in the Philistine army, stood and roared at the Israelites.

'Choose one man to come and fight me. If he beats me, then all of us will be your slaves, but if I win, you will be ours!'

Everyone was scared to death, because Goliath was nearly ten feet tall. He wore a bronze helmet and strong armour and nobody was brave enough to fight him.

One day David came to bring his brothers some food, because they were in the Israelite army. He heard Goliath and was amazed and angry that nobody would fight him. When Saul saw him, David immediately told him that *he* would fight Goliath.

'But you're just a boy!' said Saul. 'How can you fight such a giant?'

'I'm a shepherd boy,' said David. 'Every day I have to defend my flocks against lions and bears. God saves me from wild animals, so I know he can save me from this giant Philistine!'

'Go then, and may God be with you!' said Saul.

He gave David his armour and the boy tried it on, but it was much too big and heavy.

'I'll go just as I am,' said David, taking it off.

He went down to the stream and chose five smooth round stones. Then he walked out to where Goliath stood.

'Why have they sent a mere boy to fight me?' Goliath roared. 'I will kill him and feed him to the birds!'

'You come to fight with a sword, a spear and a javelin and hope to kill me!' said David. 'But I come in the name of the Lord God of Israel. He will make sure I kill you and then everyone will know that this victory belongs to God!'

David raced towards Goliath, swinging his sling above his head. The stone hit Goliath in the middle of his forehead and he dropped down dead. David ran and cut Goliath's head off with the giant's own sword.

When the Philistines saw this they ran away, followed by the cheering Israelite army.

DINAH'S STORY

My name is Dinah and my father is a horse trader. I've just become an older sister because my mother had twin boys last week. A few days later my aunt had a baby boy too, so our house is full of babies! I can't really tell them apart, but Mother and Aunt know exactly which one is which. They say that mothers can always tell their own baby. Aunt told me the story of wise King Solomon, who had to decide which baby was which, years ago. Do you know that story?

39
Wise King Solomon

David, the shepherd boy, became king and reigned for forty years. He made a lot of mistakes, but he was usually a good king. He loved music and wrote many songs of praise to God. When David was very old and frail he made his son Solomon king. One night God appeared to Solomon in a dream and offered him whatever he wanted.

'I want to be a good king, but I'm still young,' said Solomon. 'So could you please give me wisdom so I can rule your people well?'

God was pleased with this request.

'I will grant your wish,' he said, 'and because you weren't selfish when I offered you whatever you wanted, I will make you very rich and powerful too.'

Soon Solomon had to make use of his new wisdom when two women brought a baby to the king.

'We both live in the same house,' said the first woman. 'I had a baby boy recently and three days later this woman also had a son. But last night she rolled over on her baby while she was asleep and killed it. Then she took my son and put her dead baby in his place! Now she won't give him back!'

'It's not true!' said the second woman. 'It's your boy that's dead! You can't prove anything!'

Then the women began to argue and fight over the baby. King Solomon considered the problem until he had a way to find out which was the real mother.

'Be quiet!' he ordered them. 'Bring me a sword. As you can't agree whose son it really is, I shall cut the baby in two and you shall have half each!'

'All right then,' said the second woman. 'She shan't have him, so just cut him in two!'

'No, don't kill him!' begged the first woman. 'Give him to the other woman if you must, but don't kill him!'

Then King Solomon knew who the real mother was.

'Don't cut the baby in two,' he ordered. 'Give it to the first woman, because only a real mother would behave as she did.'

When the people heard of this clever way of solving the problem, they knew that wise King Solomon was truly guided by God.

LABAN'S STORY

My name is Laban and my father is a tanner in the village of Zarephath, where we live. It hasn't rained here for a very long time and everyone is praying for a miracle. But I'm sure the rain will come again, because we all believe in miracles here. I saw one happen to my best friend, Obed, who lives next door to me. It's an amazing story!

40
Elijah Saves the Widow's Son

God told Elijah the prophet to hide in a barren wilderness. There was nothing for him to eat, so every morning and night God sent down ravens with bread and meat for him. Elijah could drink from the stream, so he had everything he needed.

Then the stream dried up. God said to Elijah, 'Go to Zarephath, where I have asked a widow to give you food.'

When Elijah got to our village he found a woman and asked her for a drink of water. 'Please could I have some bread too? I'm very hungry.'

'I don't have any bread,' the woman said sadly. 'I've only got a handful of flour at home, and a little bit of oil. I'm just gathering some firewood to cook this last meal for my son and me. Then I'm sure we'll starve to death.'

'Don't worry,' said Elijah. 'Go home and cook the meal you planned. But first make me a little loaf of bread. God promises that neither your flour nor your oil will run out until rain falls again on the crops of Israel.'

The woman did exactly as Elijah had asked and God did what he promised. There was always flour in the crock and oil in the jar, no matter how much they used. Every day they had enough food to eat.

Then the widow's young son became very ill and died.

'Are you punishing me for my sins by killing my son?' the widow asked him, as she wept over the body.

'Give him to me!' said Elijah.

He carried the boy upstairs to his own room, where it was cooler, and laid him on the bed. Then he cried out to God, 'Why have you brought this sadness to the widow who has been so kind to me?'

He stretched his arms over the boy three times and prayed, 'O God, please return this child's life to him!'

God heard Elijah's prayer and the boy came back to life, so he took him back downstairs to his mother. The widow was so happy and thanked Elijah.

'Now I know for sure that you are a man of God and whatever you say comes from him!' she said.

LILAH'S STORY

My name is Lilah and I am an orphan. I survive by gathering wood in the hills. There are always bands of travellers passing by. They stop in our small village to rest their animals and make a meal each evening. I bring them wood and start their fire for them and then they share their food with me. They let me sit by the fire and listen to their stories too and that's often even better than the food.

It's easy to get a fire going with dry wood, but every time the wood is damp I remember the story of how the prophet Elijah started a blazing fire with wood that was very wet. I wish I'd been there to see it.

41
Fire from Heaven

After three years without rain God sent Elijah to tell wicked King Ahab that the drought and famine in his country was going to end. 'Not you again, you troublemaker!' said Ahab when he saw Elijah.

'It's you and your family who make trouble for Israel by worshipping the idol, Baal, instead of God,' said Elijah. 'Now bring all the people and the prophets of Baal to Mount Carmel.'

When everyone was gathered on the mountain Elijah said, 'It's time for you all to decide who to follow. We'll have a contest between me and the four hundred and fifty prophets of Baal.

'We'll sacrifice bulls and make altars to burn them on. Then we will call upon our gods. Whichever one sends fire from heaven will be the true God.'

So the prophets of Baal prepared their sacrifice and put the meat on the altar. They danced around it and called out to Baal for fire.

'Perhaps Baal is asleep!' said Elijah, when nothing had happened by midday.

By nighttime there was still no fire. Then Elijah called the people to watch him. He built an altar, put twelve big stones around it and dug a large trench around the altar.

'Bring four big pots of water and pour them on my altar!' he said.

The people poured the water on the altar so the wood and meat were soon soaking wet. Three times they refilled the pots until even the trench was full of water.

'Show the people that you are the true God and I am your servant!' Elijah prayed. 'Show them your power so they will return to you!'

Then God sent fire blazing down from heaven. It was so fierce that it burnt up all the wet wood, the meat and even the stones and licked up all the water in the trench.

Then the people believed in God again and called out, 'The Lord is the true God!'

ABE'S STORY

My name is Abe and I am the son of a chariot maker in the town of Bethel. All day I work in the smithy by the hot fire, helping my father shape iron chariots. The metal glows brightly in the light from the fire and reminds me of the story of the prophet Elijah being taken up into heaven in a chariot of fire.

42
Chariot of Fire

After many years serving God on earth, it was time for Elijah to be taken up to heaven. Another prophet, Elisha, was going to carry on his work, but he was sad to see Elijah go.

'I'm going to Bethel now,' said Elijah. 'Why don't you wait here?'

'No, I'm coming with you,' said Elisha.

When they got to Bethel the people said to Elisha, 'Don't you know that God's going to take Elijah soon?'

'Don't remind me!' said Elisha sadly.

'I'm going to Jericho next,' said Elijah. 'Why don't you stay here, Elisha?'

'Wherever you go, I'm coming with you,' said Elisha firmly and went with him to Jericho and then to the River Jordan. Here Elijah rolled up his cloak and hit the water with it. The waters divided, so they could cross to the other side.

'The time has
come for me to go,'
said Elijah. 'Is there
anything I can do for
you before I go?'

'I'm going to need
a double measure of your
spirit to do your job,' said Elisha.
'Could you give me that?'

'That's a hard one!' said Elijah. 'If you see me go,
you will know you have your wish. If you don't see me, you will not have it.'

A chariot and horses of fire appeared as he spoke and Elisha
watched in awe as Elijah was carried up to heaven in a
whirlwind.

Elisha was very sad to see him go. He picked up Elijah's
cloak and walked back to the river. He hit the water
with the cloak and the waters parted for him, just as
they had done for Elijah. He crossed the river
to where the prophets of Jordan were waiting.
They had seen everything and said to Elisha,
'The spirit of Elijah has come upon
you!'

So Elisha knew that
his last request had
been granted.

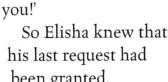
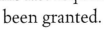

SETH'S STORY

I'm Seth and I'm a fisherman's son. When the wheat is ripe, I sneeze. When I walk through a flower-filled meadow, I sneeze. Sometimes I sneeze so many times I think my head will fall off! I'm glad I'm not a farmer's son. Out here on the lake there's nothing to make me sneeze. Instead I can think about all the stories my family tell, while we wait for the fish to swim into our nets. One of my favourites is about a rich woman's son who once sneezed seven times in a row.

43
Seven Sneezes

Elisha was often invited to eat at the home of a rich lady in Shunem. One day she said to her husband, 'Let's build an extra room on to our house, then Elisha can stay there whenever he comes to Shunem.'

Elisha visited often and was pleased at her kindness. One day he said to his servant Gehazi, 'What can I do for this good lady who has been so kind?'

'She has no son,' said Gehazi, 'and her husband is quite old.'

So Elisha said to the woman, 'This time next year when I visit, you'll have a baby son in your arms.'

The woman couldn't believe it and thought Elisha was teasing her. But within a year she was filled with joy when she gave birth to a boy, just as Elisha had told her. The boy grew to be strong and helped his father in the fields. But one day the boy had terrible pains in his head and after a few hours he died.

The rich woman laid him on Elisha's bed and rushed off to Mount Carmel to tell the prophet what had happened. He came back with her, but sent Gehazi on ahead, giving him his staff and telling him to lay it on the boy. Gehazi raced to the house and laid the staff along the boy's body, but nothing happened.

Elisha went into his room alone and found the child lying there, cold and dead. He prayed to God, then stretched his arms over the boy until he felt him begin to get warm.

He did this several times, until the boy sneezed seven times and opened his eyes. Elisha called for the child's mother, who was filled with joy as she rushed in and hugged her son.

ABNER'S STORY

My name is Abner and I work as a goatherd in the hills of Babylon. My goats are the stupidest in the world! They keep wandering into this valley looking for food and I hate going after them because there's nothing here but bones. It's a bit scary really, but I'm the youngest, so I always get sent to find them. As I stopped to rub my sore knees I saw a very strange sight. A man suddenly appeared out of nowhere. I've seen him in the village so I recognised him as Ezekiel, the priest. But how could he have just flown out of the sky like an eagle?

44
Rattling Bones

Ezekiel was a prophet who worked with the Israelites who were exiled into the foreign land of Babylon. God set Ezekiel down in the valley and showed him the dry heaps of bones.

'These aren't old animal bones!' said Ezekiel in surprise. 'They're people's skeletons! This valley is a gigantic graveyard.'

'Could these bones become alive again?' God asked him.

Ezekiel had never heard of skeletons becoming alive!

'Tell these bones that I'm going to give them muscles,

cover them with skin and make them live and breathe once more. Then they will know for sure just how powerful I am,' said God.

So Ezekiel repeated God's words. Hardly had he finished speaking when there was a loud rattling noise. The bones of each body rattled together as they attached themselves exactly as they used to be. Soon the bones were covered with muscles and skin and looked like real people again.

'Now I want you to call the winds, Ezekiel,' said God. 'Tell them to blow from every corner of the earth and breathe life into these dead bodies.'

Ezekiel ordered the winds to blow and immediately the bodies become real live men again. There were so many of them that they looked like a huge army stretching right across the valley.

Then God told Ezekiel what this meant. 'These bones stand for the people of Israel,' he said. 'They live in a foreign land, as miserable and without hope as a heap of dried-up old bones. But I will breathe new life into them just as I have into these dry bones. I will bring them home and look after them. They will become powerful again and live in peace.'

ABIGAIL'S STORY

I am Abigail, a spice merchant's daughter. I love to see the bags of spices open in my father's shop. They look like a many-coloured blanket: yellow, orange and brown, black and white and lots of shades of green. I like the smells too, many so strong they make my nose tickle.

Some customers want spices already ground when they buy them, ready to flavour their food that day, and that's a job I can do. As I grind the spices, I like to remember the stories I've heard about the faraway places some spices come from, or people who depended on them. Best of all I like the stories of Daniel, who was captured by the Babylonian king, Nebuchadnezzar.

45
Vegetables are Good for You!

When the Babylonians captured Jerusalem, they took captives back to Babylon. They chose the strongest and cleverest young Israelites to train them to work in the King's palace. Daniel and three of his friends were captured and were told they would spend three years learning to speak and write in the language of the Babylonians.

Daniel didn't mind this so much, but he didn't want to eat the same rich food the king did, or drink lots of wine. He knew that it wasn't healthy and it also contained foods forbidden by his faith.

'My friends and I don't want to eat your rich food, or drink wine', said Daniel. 'We'd like a much plainer diet. Lentils and vegetables flavoured with the spice cumin, or garlic, would be excellent. And we just want water to drink.'

'I can't do that!' said the guard. 'The king wants to fatten you up and has ordered you to eat his food. If I just gave you vegetables and water you'd grow weak and probably die. Then the king would blame me and he'd definitely kill me!'

'Vegetables are *very* healthy', said Daniel. 'Let us eat them for ten days. We could hardly die in such a short time! Then you'll see I'm right.'

So the guard let them try their new diet. After ten days they were fitter and healthier than the others who had eaten the rich food and wine. So they were allowed to eat what they wanted.

The three years passed and God gave Daniel the gift of wisdom and understanding dreams. King Nebuchadnezzar found that Daniel was cleverer than all his magicians, so he gave Daniel an important job.

ABIGAIL'S STORY

My father has been selling spices for thirty years and he knows everything about them. He told me you should never eat strongly spiced food just before you go to bed, or you will be sure to have nightmares! I think that's why King Nebuchadnezzar had such bad dreams.

46
Nebuchadnezzar's Bad Dream

King Nebuchadnezzar kept having a horrible nightmare. He didn't know what it meant so he summoned all the wise men in Babylon to explain his dream to him.

'Tell me what my dream means!' he ordered.

'Tell us about your dream first, or how can we say what it means?' they replied.

'If you are as clever as you pretend you should know without me telling you!' he insisted. 'Tell me, or you will all die!'

'Only the gods can do such things!' they protested.

King Nebuchadnezzar was so angry he ordered all the court officials to be executed, including Daniel and his friends. When Daniel heard about this he prayed to God to save their lives by telling him the king's dream and what it meant. So God gave him all the answers.

'No man is clever enough to explain your dream,' Daniel said to the king next day. 'But God knows everything and he has told me that your dream is about what will happen in the future.'

'Tell me my dream and what it means!' ordered the king.

'You saw a huge statue of a man,' said Daniel. 'Its head was gold, its body silver and its legs were bronze. Then a rock hit the statue's feet, which were made of iron and clay and broke them into many pieces. The whole statue crumbled into millions of little bits and was blown away by the wind. The rock became an enormous mountain, covering the whole world.'

'You are right,' said the king. 'But what does it mean?'

'The gold stands for your own strong kingdom,' said Daniel, 'the silver and bronze for other smaller kingdoms. The rock that destroyed everything is God's eternal king-dom. One day this will cover the whole world.'

The king realised that Daniel must be speaking the truth to know his dream without ever being told.

'Your God must truly be Lord of all!' said King Nebuchadnezzar. 'Stay here with me, Daniel, and I will reward you and make you ruler of all of Babylon!'

So Daniel made sure his friends had good jobs too, but he stayed with the king.

MEL'S STORY

My name is Mel and my father is an iron maker in the town of Bethany. Today he is making a new plough for one of the farmers nearby. He has to make the iron very hot, so it becomes soft enough to be hammered into shape. My job is to pump the bellows to make the furnace really hot. The searing heat from the furnace reminds me of the amazing story of Daniel in the fiery furnace.

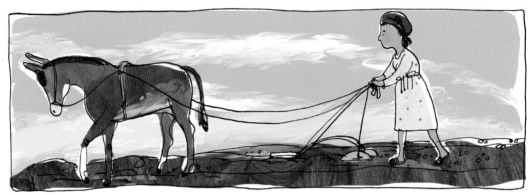

47
The Fiery Furnace

King Nebuchadnezzar made a huge golden statue and commanded all his people to come and see it.

'Every time my musicians play on their instruments, you must all bow down and worship this statue!' he ordered. 'Anyone who disobeys will be thrown into a fiery furnace!'

Nebuchadnezzar had given Daniel's three friends new names. He called them Shadrach, Meshach and Abednego. They, like Daniel, were all Jews and worshipped only God, so they refused to bow down to the statue. When the king heard about this he was very angry.

'I'll give you one more chance to bow down to my statue,' he told them. 'If you don't, your God cannot save you from the fiery furnace!'

'Our God could save us from the flames if he wished. But even if he doesn't, we won't bow down to anyone but him,' they replied bravely.

King Nebuchadnezzar was so angry that he ordered the furnace to be made seven times hotter. It was so hot that the soldiers who tied up Shadrach, Meshach and Abednego and threw them into the furnace were burnt up immediately. The king expected the three friends to be burnt up too, so he was amazed to see four men walking about in the fire.

'Who is that shining creature that looks like a son of the gods?' he asked. 'And how can they be walking about when we tied them up and threw them into such hot fire?'

King Nebuchadnezzar realised that theirs must be the true God and called them out. Shadrach, Meshach and Abednego came out of the fire. Neither their clothes nor their bodies were burnt. They didn't even smell of smoke!

'Everyone must praise their God!' said Nebuchadnezzar. 'They were willing to die rather than worship another god, but their true God sent an angel to rescue them!'

Then he promoted them all to better jobs in his kingdom.

ALVAN'S STORY

My name is Alvan and I am apprenticed to a silversmith. The other boys and I watch our master closely, for we all long to be allowed to work with the precious silver. I have been apprenticed here longest and I've seen my master make the most beautiful things, like silver jewellery set with shiny blue stones. But my favourites are the cups set into the backs of silver lions or fabulous birds. I think they are as good as the cups King Belshazzar used at his feasts!

48
The Writing on the Wall

Nebuchadnezzar's son was called Belshazzar. One day, after he had become king, he was feasting with more than a thousand of his most important officials.

'Get out the sacred gold and silver cups my father stole from the temple at Jerusalem!' he commanded. 'We'll use them to drink wine.'

They drank from the precious cups and got very drunk. Then they began to worship their idols. Suddenly the king saw human fingers appear and write on the white palace wall. It was in a strange language he didn't understand, so he called his wise men to explain. But nobody could say how fingers without an arm or a body attached could write, or what the strange words meant. King Belshazzar became very frightened.

'Call Daniel,' the queen advised. 'He'll know the answer.'

So the king asked Daniel to explain the strange writing. 'I'll make you the most powerful man in my kingdom if you can tell me,' he said.

'You don't need to reward me,' said Daniel, who only wanted to serve God. 'This is the meaning of the words. God is telling you that because you used the sacred cups to drink wine at your party, you are not fit to be king. Your kingdom will be divided between the Medes and the Persians.'

Even though this was very bad news for him, Belshazzar kept his promise, and rewarded Daniel by making him a powerful leader. That same night, God's words came true when an invading army killed King Belshazzar.

ALVAN'S STORY

As I work hard polishing the silver cup my master has just made, I think about the stories of Daniel. He was so often in danger, but he always trusted in God to protect him, even when he was thrown to the lions!

49
Danger in the Lions' Den

Darius the Mede became king after Belshazzar. He liked Daniel, but everyone else was out to get him. Daniel was a good governor and King Darius wanted to put him in charge of the whole of Babylon. This made all the other officials very jealous, so they tried to get Daniel into trouble with the king. But Daniel was honest and worked very hard, so this was a hard thing for them to do.

They tricked the king into making a law that for thirty days people could pray only to the king. They knew that Daniel prayed to God every day and they wanted him to be eaten by the lions as punishment for breaking the new law.

Despite the danger he was in, Daniel prayed to God three times every day, thanking him for his goodness. The jealous officials reported him to the king, insisting that Daniel be punished by being thrown to the lions.

King Darius was horrified because he knew Daniel was a good man, but even a king could not change a law of the Medes and Persians once it was made. So Daniel was thrown into a den of hungry, vicious lions. A big stone was put in front of the lions' cave, so Daniel could not escape.

All night long King Darius lay awake, worrying about Daniel and hoping that his God was strong enough to save him. Next morning he hurried to the den and called out, 'Daniel! Daniel! Did your God save you from the lions?'

'God sent an angel to stop the lions from eating me because he knew I'd done the right thing. I'm perfectly safe!' replied Daniel.

King Darius ordered that Daniel should be set free and the jealous officials thrown to the lions instead.

PEREZ'S STORY

My name is Perez and my father is a sea captain. We've spent all winter ashore, mending the sails and oars of his ship. I've been cleaning up the four heavy iron anchors and attaching new marker-buoys and now everything is shipshape. Soon the rainy season will be over and we can go to sea again. When there are lots of clouds we can't see the stars, so there's no way we can navigate. The sea's really rough in the winter too, so there's danger of shipwreck and losing all our precious cargo overboard. But at least we've never had a passenger aboard like Jonah!

50
Jonah and the Mighty Fish

The people of Nineveh were very wicked. So God told Jonah, the prophet, to go and tell them how angry he was and order them to stop their evil ways. But Jonah was afraid to go to Nineveh because the people were so bad. Instead he bought a ticket on a ship going in the opposite direction. He hid down in the dark hold and soon went to sleep.

But God knew exactly where he was and made a huge wind blow, so that the ship was rocked by gigantic waves. The sailors were very scared. They called out to their gods for help and threw all the cargo overboard to lighten the ship. The captain was angry when he found Jonah asleep in the hold.

'How can you sleep in a storm like this!' he shouted above the roar of the sea. 'You should be praying to your God to save our lives!'

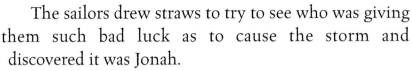

The sailors drew straws to try to see who was giving them such bad luck as to cause the storm and discovered it was Jonah.

'Who are you and what have you done to bring this great storm upon us?' they asked.

'I'm a Jew and I'm running away from my God,' admitted Jonah. 'The storm is all my fault, so the only way to stop it is to throw me overboard!'

The sailors didn't want Jonah to die, so they tried harder to row the boat ashore, but the storm just got worse and they couldn't make it. So, reluctantly, they threw him overboard, knowing he would probably drown.

The storm stopped immediately and the sailors promised to follow Jonah's powerful God for ever. Jonah sank down and down into the deep ocean.

Floating seaweed tangled itself around his body as he prayed to God to save him from drowning. Suddenly a gigantic fish opened its mouth and swallowed him whole.

Jonah stayed inside this huge fish for three days and nights. He praised God for saving his life and promised to do God's will for ever. Then God made the great fish spit Jonah up on to a beach, where he landed safe and sound.